PANDORA

by William Mayne
illustrated by Dietlind Blech

Alfred A. Knopf　New York

Pandora was a happy cat. She lived in a house. Man and woman loved her, she
could tell.

She had knees to curl up on, laps to collapse in. She stretched out by the fireside. She
shared the meals at table, sitting by the teapot in its cozy. She wore a red collar.

"Our black cat," man would say, rubbing her ears.

"Our Pandora," said woman, scratching a black chin.

"We are so happy," they all said, one and two and three of them.

Something came into the house, wrapped in a blanket and a shawl. Pandora did not know what it was – perhaps something like a teapot in its cozy. But it smelled of milk.

"Warm some up for me," she said. "It's time."

She got no milk. No one heard her, or seemed to see her.

She was not the third one at the fireside now; she was the last. The new thing in the shawl stole all the time and space and love.

When it began to squall, man jumped up and put a foot on Pandora by the fender.

When it sighed and sneezed, woman got up and kicked Pandora in the ribs.

"Accidents will happen," said Pandora. "But this is not quite as it was before."

Man said, "I'll put her outside, she's in the way."

"We don't want her near the baby," said woman. "Really."

"*Our* baby, surely," said Pandora. "We are one, *and* two, *and* three, him and her and me. And in the shawl is It."

They did not know she spoke. She was put outside; the door was closed. She jumped up to a window that was locked. She slept in the shed, a sack for a bed.

In the morning she came to table, between the teapot and the toast, her place.

"That's not nice anymore," woman said. "She smells of shed. A cat's not clean; you don't know where it's been."

"I'm clean," Pandora said. "I wash *all* over *every* day."

"Down you go," said man, pushing with his hand. "Stay on the floor."

"We have a baby now," said woman. "It's extra care."

For Pandora there was no extra care. It was hard floor for her, locked door for her; cold milk and scraps, no comfortable laps; no more love; no one and two and three of them at the fireside at night.

Pandora did not eat, or romp. Woman had the baby now and there was little for Pandora. She was an unhappy cat.

She left. All she took was her red collar.

"Goodbye," she said, but no one understood. "I am too proud to explain. I will not make a fuss. I'll live alone. I can be kind to me."

She went beyond the gardens to the woodland, and beyond the woodland to the rocks. There she found a cave beneath an oak.

"They love me, or they love me not," she said. "I do not care. I am alone, as every cat should be. I love me alone; one and one and one is ME."

She was a low black shadow in the grass, a dark mark among the bushes, as happy as Wilderness could make her. She lost her collar in the thorns.

When lightning struck, or water trickled through the cave, she thought of one and two and three, and milk warm, and the fire, curling up tighter on the bare, damp earth, while the wind fluttered in her ears.

She grew wild with the Wilderness.

When everything a cat could eat lay sleeping underground, Pandora felt the pain of hunger. She crouched in muddy places waiting for a mouse, and came to her cave hungry and hard to clean, and thought how she had sat between the teapot and the toast.

She grew hardy and strong. She had no time to be unhappy. She was wild as winter.

One night, when frost was deep and sharp, Pandora did not go to hunt. She stayed in her cave, alone, in the winter nest she made of grass.

When the moon was rising on the hill a kitten was born to her.

When the moon was high in the black oak branches there came another.

As the moon went down Pandora purred, and licked, and kept them warm.

She was their fireside, their lap. She was not alone, but one *and* two *and* three again.

Snug inside their leafy nest the kittens grew. Their eyes came blue and open and they looked.

"I love them," said Pandora. "Man and woman loved their little one too, more than anything. That is one and two and three for them, and these are the same for me."

Far beyond the rocks, far beyond the woodland, the lighted windows of the house were bright.

"I understand them now," Pandora said, sitting on the post of the garden fence. She saw man come out; she heard him shout a name she knew, Pandora.

When the kittens had strength to follow she brought
them from the hollow underneath the oak, through
the woodland to the fence, and down the garden.
They came like shadows, like black holes in the snow.

At the open door Pandora looked on light and warmth, and at what was sitting on the rug beside the fire. She forgot she had been wild and proud.

"My place," she said. "Ours." She picked up her elder kitten, crossed the threshold, and went to the hearth-rug.

The baby did not understand, and began to cry. The kitten mewed.

"Hush," said Pandora. "Hush, both."

She went to the garden once again and brought her younger kitten. On the hearth-rug now were babies one and two and three, and Pandora.

The baby stopped its cry, smiled, put out a hand, and stroked her fur. The baby laughed. Pandora began to purr. Her kittens sat beside her.

Man came in. "Hello, she's back," he told woman, and woman said, "Let baby wait.

We'll warm some milk. Our cat Pandora has come back so we shall be kind. She left because we were too busy for that."

"Welcome home," said man, rubbing her ears.

"All one family," said woman, tickling a black chin.

"I understand," said Pandora. "I've been busy too."

Now she is a happy cat; she loves so many things: two lots of one and two and three, all at the table, cozy between the teapot and the toast.

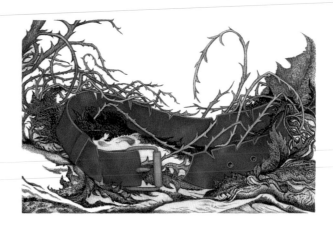

But her red collar lies forgotten among
the thorns of the Wilderness.

This story is for Olivia Amsden W. M.

For Benjamin, Liese & Frieder D. B.

THIS IS A BORZOI BOOK PUBLISHED BY ALFRED A. KNOPF, INC.

Manufactured in Hong Kong

Library of Congress Cataloging-in-Publication Data
Mayne, William, 1928–
Pandora / by William Mayne ; illustrated by Dietlind Blech.
p.   cm.
Summary: Feeling neglected when her human family has a baby, Pandora the cat runs away to live in the wild,
where she has her own kittens before returning to her house.
1. Cats—Juvenile fiction. [1. Cats—Fiction. 2. Babies—Fiction.]
I. Blech, Dietlind, ill. II. Title.
PZ10.3 M4544Pan   1995
[E]—dc20   95-21671
ISBN 0-679-84183-0   (trade)
ISBN 0-679-94183-5 (lib. bdg.)

10 9 8 7 6 5 4 3 2 1

First American Edition, 1996